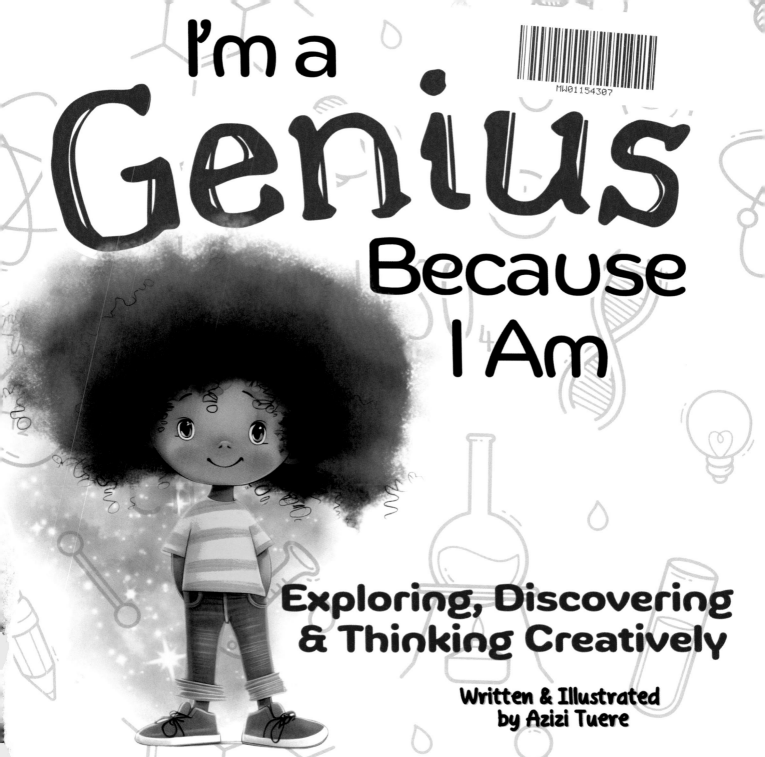

I'm a Genius Because I Am

Exploring, Discovering & Thinking Creatively

Written & Illustrated
by Azizi Tuere

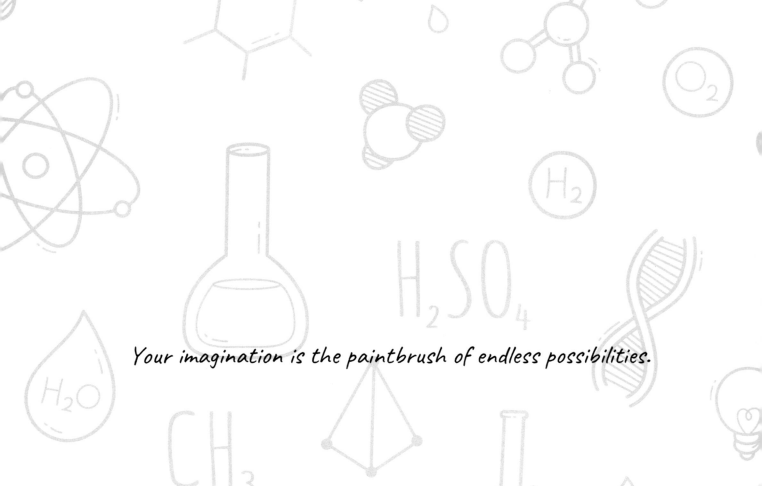

Your imagination is the paintbrush of endless possibilities.

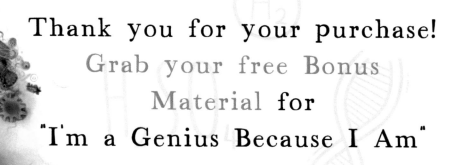

Thank you for your purchase!
Grab your free Bonus
Material for
"I'm a Genius Because I Am"

Scan me
for a free
gift

Website: go.azizituere.com/gifts

Every morning is a new day. The sunbeams peek through my window, and my 'Imagination Playground' is all set to open, to solve mysteries, and to create. There are so many ways to use my clever brain.

Oh, what an incredible day to be a genius, to be me!

I'm learning so many fun facts, flipping through cool books, and even figuring out math mysteries. But there's got to be more to being a genius than having a head full of big book stuff.

I think to myself,
"What makes me a genius?
Is it just about facts and knowing all the right answers?"

The sky isn't just blue when I look at it. I see wings, and I see myself soaring through the air. The clouds whisper, 'You're special and a genius.' But there's still so much more to explore.

I'm ready for an incredible journey! A journey to understand what makes me a genius!

I'm a genius because when I see a box, it's not just a box. I see a spaceship waiting for an intergalactic adventure!

I'm a genius because I have visions of a big world growing in my head, even when I start small. These blocks aren't just toys; they're the beginning of my mini-city.

I'm a genius because when I look at a seed, I see more than just a seed. I see a future tree, a bird's nest, and a cool spot for picnics.

I'm a genius because when I look at my box of random parts I've collected, I don't see junk. I see a chance to dive in and make something exciting and new. Who knows what I might invent?

I'm a genius because I can make stories come alive. With my puppets, I can make people laugh and feel many things straight from my mind.

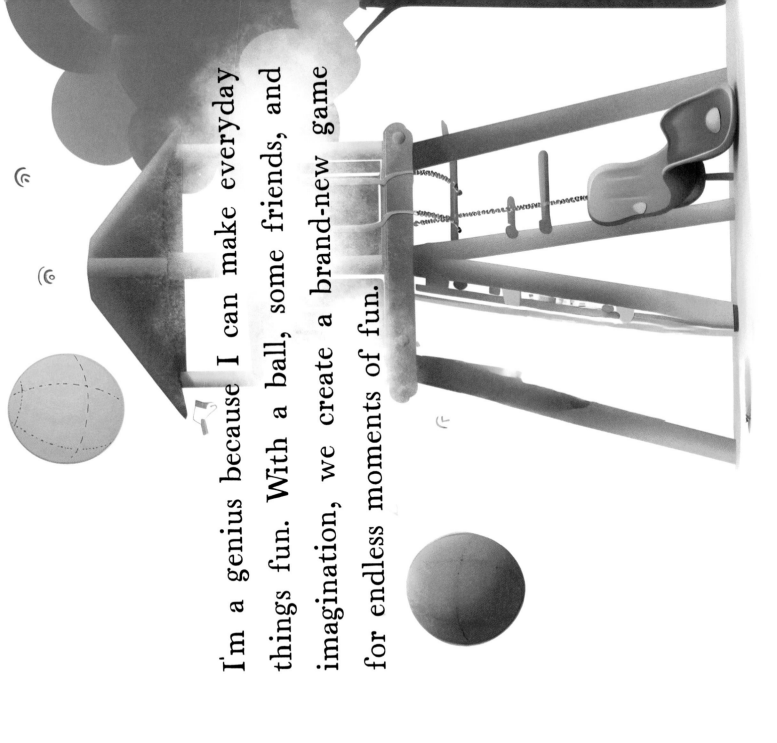

I'm a genius because I can make everyday things fun. With a ball, some friends, and imagination, we create a brand-new game for endless moments of fun.

I'm a genius because I like to try new things in the kitchen. Even if it gets a little messy. The right mix could create the yummiest treat ever!

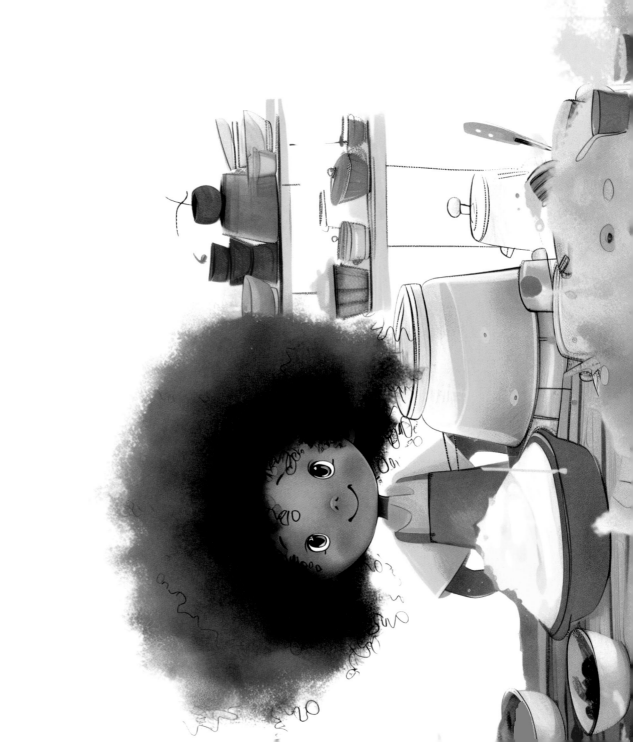

Every amazing mind, all around the world, started like me: curious, eager, and full of ideas.

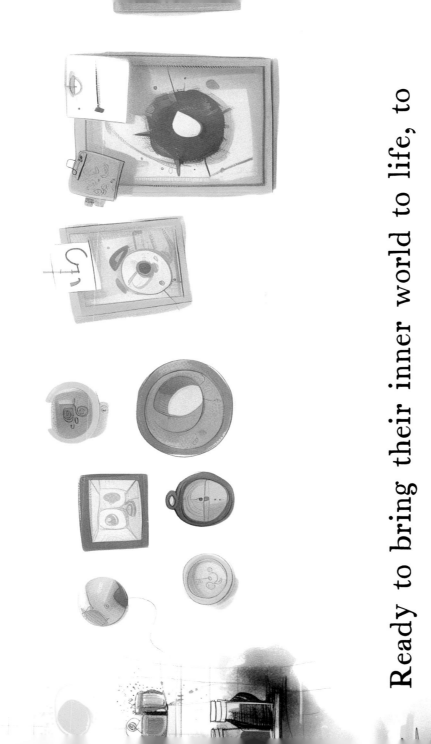

Ready to bring their inner world to life, to create their future masterpieces, to solve mysteries, and to make a difference.

I'm a genius because I am using my imagination to grow every day. Each day brings new ideas to uncover, making each night a sweet success.

Being a genius isn't about being the smartest or getting everything right; it's about exploring, dreaming, and creating.

Now I know! I'm a genius because I am...
I am me! And that's the best genius I can be.

And the adventure continues every day,

as you discover more and more about

the genius you are too.

Dear Caregivers,

I'm a Genius Because I Am seeks to ignite the innate creativity and limitless potential within every child. As you journey through these pages with your young reader here are suggestions to keep in mind:

Chat: Ask them what moments sparked their imaginative ideas.

Engage: Let real-life activities, like building something from a box, bring the story to life.

Celebrate: Together, craft your own "I am a genius because..." declarations.

Reaffirm: Regularly remind them of their unique and incredible genius.

Your partnership in fostering their self-belief and imaginative prowess is invaluable.

Warm wishes!

Thank you for your purchase! We hope you have enjoyed the book.

You can leave us an Amazon review using the web link below or by scanning the QR code. Your feedback helps us continue to create great books for everyone to enjoy!

Website link to Amazon review:

go.azizituere.com/geniusreview

Also available, or coming soon, in the series:

Meet the Author

Azizi Tuere, a lifelong storyteller, was inspired to pursue her dream of writing children's books by her twelve-year-old daughter's publishing venture. Her "Because I Am..." picture book series aims to help families grow closer and build children's self-worth through heartwarming stories.

As a homeschool mom of two young daughters, Azizi creates entertaining tales about everyday experiences that incorporate emotional intelligence. Her goal is to share positive messages with kids about their inner beauty, creativity, gratitude, and what it means to win at life.

When not writing, Azizi hosts "Tiny Green Chef," an online plant-based cooking program for kids. This initiative, like her books, provides families with practical resources to thrive together naturally.

Connect with Azizi and learn about upcoming books and projects at Azizituere.com.

www.azizituere.com

Made in the USA
Coppell, TX
07 January 2025